A QUIET STORM

A QUIET STORM

KIM SIGAFUS

7th GENERATION
Summertown, Tennessee

Library of Congress Cataloging-in-Publication Data
available upon request.

Cover and interior design: John Wincek

7th Generation
Book Publishing Company
PO Box 99, Summertown, TN 38483
888-260-8458
bookpubco.com
nativevoicesbooks.com

ISBN: 978-1-57067-415-0
E-book ISBN: 978-1-57067-804-2

Printed in the United States

28 27 26 25 24 23   1 2 3 4 5 6 7 8 9

CONTENTS

Shopping Trip Gone Wrong

CHAPTER

1

Sydney pushed back dress after dress in her closet. None of them seemed right for a formal school dance.

She was surprised her mother decided to let her go. There had been some discussion on whether or not Sydney was old enough to date, but Sydney had won out in the end, telling her they were being driven by Jeremy's mother and the dance was chaperoned. Besides, Finn was also going with them.

Sighing, she sat down on the bed. It had been six months since she and Jeremy started seeing each other. At first, her best friend, Finn, wasn't happy about the situation. He didn't trust Jeremy and tried to hover about whenever they were together at school. Sydney knew he was only trying to protect her, but she eventually had a conversation with him about backing off some. He was reluctant but did as he was asked.

Finn had been a little afraid that she wouldn't want to spend time with him anymore now that she had Jeremy, but that had not been the case. If anything, Jeremy ended up tagging along with *them* most of the time. He still hung out with his football buddies but had stopped harassing Finn, and his friends had eventually followed suit.

She wished the other bullies—like Amelia and her friends—would stop too. They had been messing with her and Finn for months, and she wondered if she would have to give a final push back to get a conclusion, good or bad, to the situation. It was obvious Finn was just trying to stay out of the way, and Jeremy didn't seem inclined to handle the issue for her.

When Finn and Jeremy weren't with Sydney, they never spent any time together. They were cautiously cordial with each other, but the friendship they had when they were younger no longer existed. They both wanted to be in Sydney's life and understood how they had to treat each other in order to be able to do so.

Sydney was aware of the uncomfortable situation but knew to stay out of it. They would either work it out or not. It was not up to her to fix it.

Since her parents' divorce and her final confrontation with her father about the way he'd treated her all her life, he had not contacted her or her mother again. While her mother was relieved, she was not. To be dumped by her father was not something she'd ever expected to happen.

"Sydney? Are you ready to go?"

Sydney frowned and slid off the bed. Her mother, Dakotah, had opened the door and was standing there with her purse.

"Go where?"

"Shopping. You need a dress, right?"

"You didn't tell me we were going shopping." Sydney smiled as she grabbed her tennis shoes and slipped them on.

"I must have forgotten. Come on, let's go."

Sydney followed her mother out to the car and buckled herself in. "Where are we going?"

"Only the biggest mall in the state," Dakotah replied with a grin. "If you can't find something there, then I give up."

"Thanks, Mom!"

They pulled out of the driveway and headed down the road. Neither spoke for a few minutes as Dakotah navigated traffic and entered the freeway.

"So, Sydney . . ."

Sydney turned to glance at her mother, but she didn't go on.

Sydney frowned. "What?"

"This is your first formal dance."

"This is my first dance, period, Mom."

"I just wondered if you had any questions about . . . well, anything." Dakotah started to blush, so she turned to glance out her driver's-side window as she moved into the left lane.

"No. I know how to dance."

"I'm not talking about dancing, Sydney. I'm talking about you and Jeremy being alone." Dakotah did not want to have this conversation, but she had no idea what her daughter knew about intimacy.

"There are other people coming to this dance, you know."

"Oh, for . . ." Dakotah cleared her throat and then let the words rush out. "I'm talking about sex, Sydney. Do you have any questions about sex?"

"What? No." Sydney blushed and looked away. "Geez, Mom . . . really?"

"Well, I don't know where you're at with these things."

"That's because we never talk about it."

"I know. That's why I thought I would bring it up now. Before the dance, you know."

"Why would you think we're going to have . . . no, Mom. Not happening. There are people there. We can't . . . I'm not going to . . ." Sydney cleared her throat. "No. I don't have any questions."

"So, you're not thinking about leaving the dance and—"

"No!"

"Okay, I just wanted to be sure."

"Okay, fine."

Dakotah sighed. "I like Jeremy."

"I know."

"I just don't want him to do anything to make me change my mind about him."

"I get it. Can we change the subject now?"

"Yes."

They pulled into the mall's large parking garage and parked. Dakotah led her daughter up the escalator and to a store that carried the kind of dresses they were looking for. She sat in a chair and watched her daughter try on dress after dress, trying to find the right one.

After about twenty minutes, Sydney pushed back the dressing room curtain and stepped out in a floor-length spaghetti-strapped satin dress.

It was red.

Dakotah frowned, but Sydney didn't catch that. She walked over to the full-length mirror and looked at herself. Dakotah cleared her throat and opened her mouth to speak, but Sydney shook her head and started to tear up.

"I . . . I look so pretty . . . ," she whispered. "I . . . I didn't know I could ever . . ." She swallowed hard and glanced over at her mother. "I look good, don't I?" she asked as she turned her gaze back to the mirror, amazed at her own image.

"Honey, you're pretty no matter what you wear, but—"

"But not like this," Sydney whispered. "Never like this."

Dakotah didn't know what to say. She thought the dress was too revealing but didn't want to burst Sydney's bubble of happiness.

"How much is it?" she asked, and her daughter frowned and fumbled for the tag. She found it and then sighed.

"Never mind," Sydney mumbled as her eyes dropped to the floor. "It's . . . it's a lot. I'll go find something else that will do."

She started for the dressing room again, and her mother sighed. Dakotah knew she was about to give in despite her better judgment.

"It might get chilly," she said, getting up and walking over to her daughter. "You might need a wrap or shawl."

She pushed Sydney back to the mirror, and they stood looking into it, each feeling different things.

"I have that shawl Nokomis gave me," replied Sydney. "The embroidered one."

Dakotah nodded. "That would look beautiful on you. Your grandmother would be honored for you to wear it at your first dance."

"But, Mom, the dress costs too much."

Dakotah looked into her daughter's soft eyes and looked down at the dress again. It was way too grown-up for Sydney, she thought. And she wasn't ready for "grown-up" Sydney.

She sighed. But Sydney was ready for "grown-up" Sydney. As much as she hated to admit it, her daughter was becoming a woman. The sooner she dealt with that, the better for both of them.

"What are you going to do with your hair?" she asked, and Sydney frowned.

"Mom, the price . . ."

"Let me see the big picture, and then I'll decide."

Sydney turned back to the mirror. "Well," she said thoughtfully, "I thought maybe I would wear it up. It's grown out a little now."

"Yes, with cascading curls, and—"

Sydney laughed. "Do I look like a 'curls' kind of girl to you?"

"Indulge me and I'll buy the dress."

"Really?" Sydney caught her breath and hugged her mother. "Yes! I will let you curl my hair. I'm so excited."

Dakotah watched her twirl around in her dress and turn from side to side to look at herself. The dress slid around her body and fit like a glove. She shone as the light hit the material, but it was the light in her eyes that caught Dakotah's attention. She wondered what Jeremy would think when he saw her.

"Okay, Sydney, go take off the dress so we can pay for it and go get some lunch."

Sydney smiled and did what she was told. Ten minutes later, Sydney and her mother walked out of the store with the dress over Sydney's arm.

CHAPTER 2

The Encounter

Sydney and Dakotah went to the food court and got some Chinese food from a popular chain. As Sydney headed for a table, Amelia, one of the bullies at school, stepped in her way. Sydney almost dropped her food but caught the tray just in time to right her drink, which had almost fallen off. She glanced behind her, but her mother was still at the counter paying for their food.

"What are you doing here?" asked Amelia.

"It's none of your business."

"Well, you can't be shopping."

"Why not?"

"Because with the clothes you wear, it's obvious you don't have any money."

Sydney shook her head. "Amelia, shut up and get out of my way."

"I don't think so." Amelia stepped closer. "Who are you to tell me what to do? You're nothing."

"Get away from my daughter."

Amelia's eyes widened as Sydney's mother came up to them. She was carrying her tray and the dress they had just bought. She sidestepped Sydney to put down her tray and turned to face Amelia.

"I know who you are, Amelia," she said, eyeing the girl up and down. "Stay away from my daughter."

Amelia took a step back. "I don't know what you're talking about. We're friends, and—"

"No, we're not," said Sydney, shaking her head.

Dakotah took another step toward the girl. "I also know who your parents are. Stay away from my daughter, or they will get brought into this. I know what you have been doing to Sydney and Finn. The school has a 'no tolerance' policy for bullying. If you want to stay in that school, I suggest you back off, or there will be consequences."

"How do you know my parents?" Amelia shrugged arrogantly and smiled. "I doubt you all run in the same circles."

"I certainly hope not," said Dakotah, "if they are anything like you. Let's see what the school has to say, shall we? I have the number right here in my phone. I happen to know Mr. Leehan is working in his office today."

At the mention of the assistant principal's name, Amelia's face paled. She dropped her gaze and stepped back.

She glared at Sydney before turning away and leaving.

Sydney sighed and sat down, and her mother set the dress over the spare chair and sat down as well.

"That didn't go well," said Sydney. "Do you really have the school's number in your phone?"

"Nope."

"Shame on you, Mom."

"Yeah, I feel so bad about lying."

"You do not."

"Nope."

Sydney shook her head, and they started eating. It was a moment before she spoke. "You shouldn't have lied, Mom. Things will get worse now at school. She's not going to let this go."

Dakotah sighed. "I'm sorry. But she made me mad, and I was not going to sit there and let her talk to you like that. Not while I'm around. I think it's time to go to the principal about all this."

"Mom . . ."

"It's been going on a while, right?"

"Well, yeah."

"It's not getting better?"

"Well, not really, but—"

"It's time, Sydney."

"But that will drag Finn into this."

"So? He's being bullied too."

"Yes, but his mother might have to get involved."

"And?"

"His mother doesn't live with them."

"Oh. So, he lives with his father?"

"Yes. His mother doesn't like Finn's . . . choice . . . so she left."

"What choice?"

"The fact that he's gay."

"She left because of that?"

Sydney sighed and put her fork down. "Yes. I told you all this before. They don't have much of a relationship."

"Does he want one?"

"I don't know," Sydney admitted. "I'm trying to stay out of it."

"Good girl. I see you learned something from the last time you stuck your nose in where it didn't belong."

"Mom . . ."

"Look, how about if I call Finn's dad and see what he says? It's about time I met the man anyway. He's been giving you rides home quite a bit."

"I guess that would be okay," said Sydney. "At least Finn wouldn't be blindsided."

They started eating again in silence, each in their own thoughts. Sydney wondered what Finn was going to think about coming forward with her to talk to the principal about being gay and all the trouble people had been giving him about it. He wasn't going to like it.

Dakotah glanced at her daughter's pensive face. She was a little pensive herself. Usually Roger, her ex-husband, handled all this stuff, but now she was on her own. She just hoped she didn't screw it up.

Finn's Dad

Sydney was nervously brushing her hair when she heard someone pull into their driveway in the back of the house.

Her mom was meeting Finn's father for the first time, and except for her dad, there hadn't been any adult company since they moved into the house.

She walked into the living room and paused, waiting for the knock at the door. It was a sparse room, with just a couch and TV. The tired-looking brown carpet was in stark contrast to the lime-green sofa her mother had gotten from one of her friends at the rez before she moved. It was used but worked fine for the two of them. Now it looked frumpy with its sagging cushions and stains here and there. Her father had liked fancy new things, but to stop further arguments, her mother had left everything to him in the divorce—which meant, of course, that they had to start over setting up their new house.

15

The house reminded her of something Nokomis, her grandmother, had said about not judging a book by its cover. Sydney's house looked great on the outside but was a mess on the inside, just like she was.

The house had been expensive, and the bills were higher than when they lived on the rez. Her dad had made the money, and he'd taken care of everything. Now it was just her mother trying to support them, and it was a little scary.

She sat on the arm of the couch and sighed as thoughts of her father drifted through her mind. She was sad he didn't seem to want her anymore, and wondered why she wasn't good enough to love. Her mother had told her it wasn't her fault, but in the back of her mind, she wondered if she had done something differently, then maybe she wouldn't feel as though she had split up her parents' marriage. It must be her fault, she reasoned, since their fights seemed to always be over how she was being raised.

The sharp knock at the kitchen door jolted her out of her thoughts, and she heard her mother walk down the hall in her bare feet.

Dakotah plastered a smile on her face as she stepped forward to open the door. Sydney stood behind her.

Finn stood in the doorway, grinning, and Sydney smiled back. Then she glanced up at Finn's dad.

He was the older version of Finn. He had short, unruly blond hair that curled up at the ends, and he wore jeans and a pressed white shirt. His eyes were smiling.

"Hi," he said, grinning down at Dakotah and extending his hand. "I'm Benjamin."

Sydney stepped forward. "This is my mother, Dakotah."

They shook hands. "Sounds very Western," Benjamin said.

Dakotah nodded. "Your name sounds very Finnish."

He laughed. "It is."

"I'm Native."

"Yes, I see that," he replied, noting her long black hair and brown complexion. He gestured to Sydney. "You have a great daughter. She has a good head on her shoulders."

"Thank you. Your son has done wonders for Sydney."

"Mom!" Sydney protested.

Benjamin nodded. "They are good for each other," he said.

"Would you like a drink?" she asked. "I have lemonade or coffee or—"

"We'll take lemonade," answered Sydney. "And Finn and I are going outside."

"I'll take coffee," said Benjamin.

Once everyone had a drink in their hand, the teenagers left out the back door and Dakotah led Benjamin to the kitchen table, where they sat down across from each other. She picked up the plate of bannock and offered him some. He took it, biting into the flat bread.

"Raisins . . . I love them," he said with a smile. "I've had something similar to this but not quite this texture."

"It's bannock," she said. "It's a kind of bread and is pretty much a staple in this house. Sydney loves it."

"I can see why."

Dakotah cleared her throat. "I thought it was important we get together and talk about the issues with the kids. They're both being bullied in school. It's been going on a long time, and I wonder if it isn't time to get involved. It needs to come to an end."

Benjamin nodded as he chewed.

"I think we should go to the principal about this," added Dakotah. "He should be able to do something." When Benjamin didn't speak, she frowned. "Do you not agree?"

He sighed. "It's not that simple. And there's no guarantee it will stop if we try to step in. We may be adding fuel to the flames."

"Well, we can't just sit back and do nothing."

"Sometimes that's the best way to handle things," Benjamin said and took a drink of coffee. "Let the kids handle it themselves."

Dakotah leaned forward, arms folded on the table. "But they can't. It's been going on too long, and—"

"There's no easy answer."

"I think there is!"

He shook his head. "Finn doesn't want me involved. I'm trying to respect his wishes."

"Sometimes they don't know what's best."

"And sometimes they do."

Dakotah sat back and shook her head. "How can you just sit back and let this happen to Finn?"

Benjamin's eyes clouded over. "It's the hardest thing I've ever had to do," he admitted quietly. "But Finn's been through enough in the last few years. I don't want to add to his suffering."

"What if we could relieve his suffering?"

"Getting involved does not guarantee that," he pointed out. "Can you promise me that we can fix this situation, and no one gets hurt? The teasing and bullying stop?"

"Well, no, but we have to try."

"What if it gets worse? What if he gets hurt . . . really hurt? They already almost took his eye out with a rock. And what about Sydney? How does she feel about you getting involved?"

"She's not thrilled about it," admitted Dakotah. "But I'm her parent. I must fix this."

"You can't fix everything."

"But I can try!"

"Mom? Is everything all right?"

Dakotah turned to see Sydney and Finn standing in the doorway.

"The kitchen window is open," Sydney reminded her.

Dakotah had forgotten that, and she sat back in her seat, sighing. Of course, they had heard everything being said, and it was a conversation she had wanted to have privately.

As Sydney waited for an answer from her mother, Finn glanced at his dad.

Benjamin was sitting quietly, holding his coffee cup in his hand. He looked up and smiled at Dakotah. "Dinner."

"What?" Dakotah frowned. "Huh?"

"Let's go out to dinner."

Dakotah's eyes narrowed. "Are you asking me out on a date? Look, I barely know you, and—"

"Don't flatter yourself," he replied, raising his eyebrows and shaking his head. "I'm not even sure if I like you or not."

"Well, then I don't understand."

"Let's take the kids out to dinner and discuss this with them. Maybe we can all come to some agreement on what should be done."

"Oh, I don't know . . ."

"Do you have plans?"

"When?"

"For dinner. Tonight. In a few hours." He frowned at her blank stare. "What's the matter? Am I going too fast for you?"

"Yes! I mean, no. I mean—"

"Dinner tonight at six. Meet me at Rosino's. They have great pizza there. I'd pick you up, but I wouldn't want you to think this was a date." He grinned, and Finn laughed.

Sydney's eyes narrowed as she waited for her mother to answer.

Frowning, Dakotah struggled with how to respond. She really didn't want to go. Benjamin was waiting for an answer though, so she glanced at Sydney, who shrugged.

"I guess that would be all right," Dakotah replied reluctantly.

Benjamin nodded and got up, and he and Finn headed for the door. A minute later, Dakotah and Sydney were watching them back out of the driveway. Sydney shot her mother a sideways glance.

"So, what did you think of Finn's dad?"

"He's okay."

"Just okay?"

"I don't know him that well," Dakotah said, pulling the door shut.

"Did you like him?"

Dakotah shrugged. "I guess. Like I said, I don't know him."

Sydney frowned at her mother and then turned to go. "I've got homework," she said. "Talk to you later."

Sydney went down the hall and opened her bedroom door. She glanced back at her mother.

Dakotah was standing in the kitchen in the same spot Sydney had left her a moment ago. She was staring out the kitchen window pensively, her hands shoved in her pockets.

Sydney opened her mouth to speak but then shut it. With a frown, she went into her room and closed the door.

Pizza and Pride

S ydney asked her mother to leave early for dinner, so they headed out the door with twenty minutes to spare. The restaurant was only five minutes away.

Finn and his dad had already arrived and were waiting for them at a table.

Sydney sat across from Finn, who was downing his drink.

"Slow down," said his father. "I'm not buying you a whole keg of pop. I want you to eat some dinner."

Finn set the glass down and grinned at Sydney. "You'll share, won't you?" he asked her and laughed when she shook her head.

"You're on your own," she declared.

The waitress showed up to get Sydney and Dakotah's drink order and then left. Dakotah nodded over at Benjamin.

"Thanks for inviting us," she said.

23

"Of course. What kind of pizza do you like?"

"Are we getting pizza?" asked Sydney.

"I thought so," said Benjamin. "They have the best in town."

"Oh."

"Did you want something else, Sydney?" asked her mother. "You can have whatever you like."

"No, that's all right. Finn and I will have a sausage and mushroom pizza."

"*You* will have a sausage and mushroom pizza," replied Finn, sitting back. "*I* am having a Hawaiian pizza."

"I thought you liked sausage and mushroom," protested Sydney. "I thought we could share one."

"Well, we can still share one," conceded Finn. "But it will be Hawaiian."

"But—"

Benjamin put a hand up. "We'll get two pizzas, one of each." He turned to glance at Dakotah. "Will that work for you?"

She nodded.

"Good, because I'm buying," he declared.

"Wait," said Dakotah, "you don't have to."

"I know, but I am."

The waitress came over with the girls' drinks and took their pizza order. Then they all settled in.

"Did you get your math homework done?" Sydney asked Finn, then took a drink of orange pop.

He shook his head. "I'm stuck on problem two."

"Why didn't you ask me for help?" asked his father, frowning.

"You weren't home. Sydney tried explaining it over the phone, but—"

"Finn, I'm an accountant. I think I can help with your math."

"Dad, you weren't *home*. Besides," added Finn with a grin, "Sydney is a whiz at math. It's her best subject."

"It is?" Dakotah frowned. "Since when?"

"Since I am acing all my tests," replied Sydney, sitting back with a grin.

"When did that start happening?"

"Last month when Benjamin started helping me with my math."

Dakotah shot Finn's dad a look. "You're tutoring my daughter?"

"No, not really," Benjamin said, leaning forward with his arms on the table. "She called to talk with Finn about a math problem, and he wasn't home." He shrugged. "I told her I could help her, and I did."

"He explains things so I can understand," said Sydney. "It was a big help. The rest I figured out on my own."

"Good for you, Sydney," Benjamin said with a smile, and Dakotah sat back with a frown. Why didn't she know about all this? Apparently, things were happening around her without her knowledge.

"Mom? Is everything okay?" asked Sydney, and Dakotah looked up to see everyone staring at her.

"Ah, yes. I was just thinking." She leaned forward and cleared her throat. "I believe we're here to talk about the situation at school."

"I'm not."

Everyone turned to Finn, who was holding his glass and swirling the ice around.

"Things are bad enough without you guys getting involved." He lifted the glass to drop an ice cube into his mouth, then started crunching it. "Sydney and I agree that we should leave well enough alone."

"We do?" asked Sydney. "I don't remember talking about this with you recently."

"I thought we were on the same page here," Finn said. "We were going to handle it ourselves. You don't let them get to you anymore, and you told Amelia off."

"Wait, what?" asked Dakotah. "When was this?"

"A while back, Mom. Look, Finn," said Sydney, "we should probably listen to what the adults have to say."

"Why?"

"Because they might have some ideas we haven't thought about. We could always use a fresh perspective."

Finn sighed. "I guess," he replied reluctantly. "But, Sydney, is anything we do going to matter to those people? I mean, you were one of them. You should know."

Sydney caught her breath.

Her mother frowned. "Finn, really. I don't think dragging up the past is a good idea . . ."

"What's this?" Benjamin asked. "Apparently, you all know something I don't." He turned to look at his son. "And that was a bit snarky, wouldn't you say?"

Everyone turned to Sydney. She glanced around at all of them and then opened her mouth to speak.

She closed it again. Mumbling something about the restroom, she quickly got up and pushed her chair back. Finn could see the pain in her eyes as she stumbled over her mother's chair, heading for the bathroom.

"Sydney, what in the world . . . ," Dakotah protested, but Sydney ignored her and strode away quickly.

Finn sighed and pushed his chair back. "I'll go," he said. "I'm the one with the big mouth."

"You're going to the girls' bathroom?" asked Dakotah.

"Obviously I'll wait outside," replied Finn, shaking his head and walking away.

Heading to the back of the restaurant, he watched Sydney disappear into the restroom. He sighed and walked over to lean against the wall across from the ladies' room.

Dakotah and Benjamin watched him, and then Benjamin turned to her and caught her eye.

"I think someone needs to tell me what's going on here," he said firmly, "and since you are the only one here, it has to be you."

Dakotah glanced in the direction her daughter and Finn went in. Then she looked over at Benjamin, who was sitting with his arms crossed, waiting for her to speak.

She shook her head and then closed her eyes, rubbing her temples. "It's a long story," she mumbled, and he nodded.

"It usually is," he stated.

"Look, I hardly know you . . ."

"Now's the time to change that."

"Why?"

He leaned forward. "We need to come clean here. I have a feeling this situation is more complicated for Sydney than I thought."

"It is," Dakotah admitted.

"Then tell me."

"It's none of your business!" Dakotah sat back, exasperated now. She didn't want to air her dirty laundry all over the place.

"Look, it might help to talk about it," he said quietly.

"I don't want to. I don't even know you."

"Look, this single-parent thing is hard enough without trying to do it on your own."

"So?"

"So . . ."

Dakotah sighed as she weighed her options. She *was* getting tired of dealing with stuff on her own. But she had just met him and wasn't even sure she *liked* him, let alone trusted him with private stuff.

Benjamin sat back with a sigh. "Look, we need to get on the same page here if we're going to help the kids."

Dakotah nodded. "Yeah, I get that."

Benjamin smiled. "So out with it then. Why is Sydney so upset?"

Dakotah hesitated for a moment and then started talking.

Almost Friends

S ydney and Finn came back to see their parents laughing and smiling at each other. Finn had managed to smooth things over with Sydney but knew she was unhappy with him for bringing up the subject of her bullying. She was still touchy about it, because she was wrestling with her past.

For the moment, he pushed those thoughts away as he glanced over at his father.

"So, what are you two talking about?" asked Finn.

"Life, son . . . just life," Benjamin answered, smiling over at Dakotah.

She nodded and smiled back.

Sydney looked at Finn and shrugged. At that moment the pizza showed up, and everyone dug in.

A few minutes later, Sydney caught Benjamin giving her mother a warm smile. She glanced at her mother and caught her smiling back. As Finn leaned over to ask his dad something, she leaned over to whisper to her mother.

"Mom, what's going on between you and Finn's dad?"

"Nothing."

"Then what's with the smiling business? You guys are flirting."

Dakotah's eyes widened. "We are not!" she hissed back.

"It sure looks like you are."

"Oh, for gosh sakes, Sydney. I hardly know the man."

"It seems like you have a thing for him."

Dakotah frowned. "What? No. I'm just trying to be nice."

"That's all?"

"Of course. Now stop whispering, or they will want to know what we're talking about."

Before Sydney could continue her line of questioning, Dakotah addressed Finn.

"Look, Finn," she said, catching his eye. "I know things are rough right now with your mom being out of the picture and your relationship not the best, but you have to know what is happening at school is not okay in any sense of the word. I think the principal needs to be brought into this. It has to stop. I know I don't want my daughter going through this, and I'm sure your dad wants the best for you after everything you've had to deal with."

Finn glanced at his father, who avoided his gaze. "What did you tell her, Dad?"

His father sighed and cleared his throat. "I thought it was best for everything to be out in the open. She really does have your best interests at heart, son. I think we should hear her out."

Finn stared at Sydney. "What do you know about this?"

She shook her head. "This is the first I'm hearing anything."

"I feel like I'm being ganged up on," grumbled Finn, putting down his pizza and sitting back.

"Please don't feel that way," replied Dakotah, and Benjamin nodded.

"Yes, we are just talking," he said. "No one has made any decisions. We're here to try to help."

"I think we're doing just fine. Don't you, Sydney?" asked Finn, leaning forward now.

Sydney hesitated. "I guess so," she answered. "I mean, the football players leave you alone now."

"Yes, but what about Amelia and her friends?" asked Dakotah. "I know they are still bothering you, Sydney, considering what happened in the mall the other day."

"What happened in the mall, Sydney?" asked Finn.

Sydney glanced at her mother and sighed. "Just regular stuff. I talked to Amelia, and—"

"Amelia needs a stern talking to," said Dakotah. "She started harassing Sydney in the food court."

"What?" asked Finn. "Why didn't you tell me that?"

Sydney shrugged. "I took care of it." She glanced at her mother. "Or rather, *she* took care of it."

"What did you do?" asked Benjamin.

"I told her to leave Sydney alone or I would be talking to the assistant principal about the situation."

"Well, what did she say to that?" asked Finn.

"Nothing," answered Sydney. "She left."

"Oh, man. That will get all over school."

Dakotah frowned at Finn. "What will?"

"How Sydney's *mommy* had to step in and rescue Sydney from Amelia. She'll be the laughingstock of the whole school."

"Finn, that was rude," said Benjamin. "Don't talk to her like that."

Finn shook his head. "You have no idea, Dad. These kids are brutal when they don't like you."

Dakotah said a nasty word, and Sydney frowned.

"Mom, stop swearing. You're embarrassing me."

Dakotah sighed. "I'm sorry. I just don't know what I'm doing here." She threw up her hands and shook her head. "Apparently, I just made it worse! And this"—she indicated everyone at the table—"is getting us nowhere."

"What do you mean?" asked Benjamin.

"I mean, what is this dinner for? What is it accomplishing anyway? You have no answers, I have no answers, how I handle things is wrong, and I don't know what to do anymore!" Dakotah stood up. "Sydney, let's go. I'll just have to figure it out on my own."

Sydney didn't move, and to Dakotah's irritation, Benjamin shook his head.

"You're overreacting," he said with a sigh.

"No, I am not," she said, pulling herself up taller and staring down at him. "I just know a dead end when I see one."

"Really? I disagree. Why don't you sit down so we can figure this out? This affects both of our kids, you know. You're too hotheaded, and this situation is calling for a calm mind."

"Oh, geez. You're not one of those yoga people, are you?" asked Dakotah as she dropped to her seat. Her purse was still on her lap.

"You have something against calm people?" Benjamin sat back and regarded her seriously. "I think I know what the problem is here. You and Sydney are too much alike."

Dakotah's eyes narrowed.

"What? No, we're not!" Sydney protested. "I'm nothing like her."

"Yes, you are, and it's a good thing most times," said Finn.

Sydney turned to glare at him. He had grabbed her drink and was finishing it off. She snatched it back, and he grinned.

"If anyone is like their parent, you are," she pointed out.

Benjamin laughed. "That could be so," he said, glancing at his son. "But anyway, we need to figure out a plan to deal with the bullying situation that makes us all comfortable." He glanced pointedly at Dakotah's purse, which was still in her lap. "I assume you would like in on this conversation?"

Dakotah sighed. Frustrated as she was, he was right. She dropped her purse on the floor under the table and grabbed a piece of pizza.

"Fine," she said, taking a bite of lukewarm food.

"Fine," repeated Benjamin. "Now let's get down to business."

The Other Man

Dakotah put the finishing touches on Sydney's hair. It was swept up to one side, with a sparkly comb holding it there. Soft curls finished the hairdo, and Sydney smiled as she stared at herself in the mirror.

Dakotah sat back to view her work. Sydney looked like a vision in red. "Oshkiniiigikwe," as Nokomis would say. A young woman.

"Mom, what do you think?" asked Sydney, catching her eye in the mirror.

Dakotah shook her head. "Miika. You look so beautiful. You are growing up too fast, nindaanis."

Sydney gave her a hug and then turned back to view herself in the mirror. "I think I will wear a little makeup," she decided.

Dakotah gave her a kiss on the top of the head and got up from her chair. "When is Jeremy arriving to pick you up?"

"In a half hour."

"Okay. Well, remember, I will want to take pictures first."

"I know."

Dakotah had turned to go, but the wistful tone of Sydney's voice made her pause. "What's wrong?" she asked, leaning against the doorframe.

Sydney shrugged. "I was just thinking about Dad."

"What about him?"

"He's missing a lot of my life."

"That was his choice."

"Maybe."

"What do you mean by that?"

Sydney caught her mother's stare in the mirror. "It takes two to tango."

Her mother crossed her arms. "Are you saying you blame me for the divorce?"

Sydney knew that tone of voice and didn't want to go down that road. "I'm saying I miss him."

Dakotah sighed. She didn't miss him, but then again, Sydney loved him and he was her father.

"I miss the dad I wanted him to be," Sydney said quietly, and Dakotah went over and wrapped her arms around her. Sydney closed her eyes against the sudden tears that threatened to fall. Her mother kissed her on the top of the head and held her.

The doorbell rang. Sydney's eyes flew to her mother's, and Dakotah smiled.

"I'll hold him off a bit," she said, and Sydney relaxed.

"I won't be long," she said and reached for her makeup.

Dakotah went to the front door and opened it to see Finn standing there, grinning. She smiled back and stepped aside to let him in.

"She's not ready yet, is she?" he asked, and Dakotah shook her head. "She's dressed though, right? Can I go in and talk to her?"

"I think that would be all right."

Finn nodded and headed for Sydney's bedroom.

"Finn."

He turned to glance at her.

"Should anything happen tonight with Amelia—" Dakotah started to say, but Finn cut her off.

"I know. I remember the plan. First ask to be left alone, and if that doesn't work, we find Mr. Leehan." He didn't like the plan, but his father had made him promise there would be no issues tonight or he would come up to the school himself.

She nodded, and he quickened his pace down the hall to Sydney's room. He stopped in the doorway, leaning against it as he stared at Sydney.

Sydney was putting on some lip balm that tinted her lips red. She put it down and turned to look at him.

His hair was neatly combed, and he was wearing a black suit with a white shirt. His shoes had black-and-white designs on them.

"Well, don't you look fancy," she said with a smile.

He shook his head. "You look beautiful, Sydney. Jeremy is going to fall all over himself when he sees you."

Sydney's smile got bigger. "Let's just hope he doesn't dance like that," she said, and Finn laughed.

"No one dances as well as I do," he said, striking a dance pose.

Sydney grinned. "Well, no one dances *like* you do, that's for sure."

Finn gave her a look as he stepped into the room and sat down on the bed. "I appreciate you guys letting me go with you tonight."

Sydney got up to head to her closet for the shawl she was going to wear. "It's no big deal," she said, pulling the shawl out and carefully examining it. "We're the three amigos, remember?"

"Yeah, well, I'm not so sure Jeremy appreciates me hanging out with you guys all the time."

Sydney glanced over at him. "He knew how things were from the start. You're my best friend."

"I just think he would like some time alone with you once in a while."

"He gets that often enough," replied Sydney, sliding the shawl over her shoulders. Finn got up to help her straighten it. "And he never complains about you being with us."

Finn sighed and shuffled his feet.

Sydney glanced over at him. "What is it?" she asked, and he shrugged. "Finn . . ."

He sighed again and then looked up at her. "If you guys . . . you know . . . want to be alone tonight . . . I mean, I can call Dad for a ride home. If you guys want to . . . you know . . . go somewhere after the dance."

"Jeremy's *mother* is driving us tonight," she reminded him.

"Lots of kids leave early and go off somewhere and then come back later."

She frowned. "Where did you hear that?"

He shrugged. "I hear people talk."

"Where are they going?" asked Sydney.

"Really, Sydney. Come on. You know the answer to that," replied Finn with a frown. "They want to be alone."

"Oh . . . I see. Well, that's not going to happen tonight. We're going there together and coming home together."

"I just don't want to get in the way."

"Finn, Jeremy and I are not in that place yet."

"Are you sure? Because I could make myself scarce, and—"

"No, Finn."

"Really? Because—"

Sydney turned to face him as the doorbell rang again. "Finn, Jeremy and I are not that physical yet. I'm not ready and he knows it. Now, let's go and have some fun tonight, okay?"

Finn nodded and then smiled. "Okay," he said. "Let's go."

Finn followed Sydney into the living room. He hung back so she could greet Jeremy on her own.

Nervously, Sydney brushed her hand down her dress and messed with her hair. Then she went to the door and opened it.

Jeremy was in a sapphire-blue suit and had gotten a haircut. His mouth dropped open as he looked Sydney up and down.

"Wow . . ." he said, trailing off for a moment. "You look good. I mean, I like your dress." Jeremy shook himself a little and then added, "It's . . . you're beautiful."

Sydney smiled bashfully. "Thanks," she said and stepped aside so he could enter.

Her mother picked that time to come in from the kitchen. She surveyed the group and then smiled. "Come on," she said. "Gather together by the door so I can get some pictures."

Obediently, the three moved over to the door, with Sydney between the two boys. They smiled on cue and then stood there for a moment as Dakotah took several pictures. Then they turned to go.

Jeremy's mother smiled as they walked toward her. She was standing outside the car and gestured for Finn to get into the front passenger seat.

"You look beautiful, Sydney," she said warmly, and Sydney gave her a shy smile.

"Thank you," she answered as Jeremy opened the door for her.

Ten minutes later, they were walking in the school's front door.

Jeremy surveyed the room and then turned to Sydney. "Do you want something to drink, or do you want to dance?"

"I could use something to drink first," she replied.

"Okay."

Sydney watched him head to the refreshment table and then turned to glance at Finn. He was nervously messing with his shirt collar.

"What's the matter?" she asked, frowning.

"What? Nothing," answered Finn, dropping his hand to his side. "I just don't know what to do next. I mean, you guys will want to dance eventually. Maybe we should find some place to sit. I'll probably be there a while."

Sydney shook her head. "What do you mean? I'll dance with you, you know."

"Yeah, but . . ." Finn trailed off for a moment and then added, "I just wish . . ."

"I know."

"You do?"

"Of course."

He sighed. "It's hard to be alone. You have Jeremy."

"I'm sorry," Sydney replied, reaching out to squeeze his hand. Glancing around the room, she noted that everyone was either dancing or sitting in groups and talking. Sydney's gaze moved back to Finn's face, and she read the sadness in his eyes. "Let's go find a table," she said, taking him by the arm.

Jeremy was headed for them with three drinks and saw them walking to the left toward an empty table. He followed a few feet behind, careful not to drop the drinks.

Finn pulled out Sydney's chair with a smile. Jeremy watched her sit down and take Finn's hand, smiling back at him.

For a moment, Jealousy hit Jeremy in the gut. She was his girl, after all, and he didn't like always having to share her with Finn. But as he approached them, he remembered how he had treated her in the beginning and how she had looked past that.

She saw something special in Finn too. She had that ability to see past someone's outer shell to peer inside them. So, with that in mind, he resolutely pushed the jealousy aside.

Jeremy set the drinks down in front of them. Finn nodded and reached out for his as Sydney smiled up at Jeremy. He sat down on the other side of her and smiled back.

One of Sydney's favorite ballads came out of the speakers, and Jeremy asked her if she wanted to dance. She nodded, and soon they were in each other's arms in a sea of other couples swaying to the music.

Finn watched for a moment and then took a drink of his punch. Suddenly, someone bumped into his chair, and the punch sloshed down the front of him. He jumped up and watched pink liquid soak his white shirt and land on his shoes.

Changes

Sydney closed her eyes as she wrapped her arms around Jeremy. They didn't do any fancy dancing. They just swayed back and forth to the soft beat of the music. Jeremy smiled and held her tighter as he laid his head next to hers.

"Thanks for letting Finn come with us," Sydney whispered in his ear. "I know you probably weren't too excited to bring him on our date."

Jeremy pulled back to look into her eyes. "To be honest, I wish we had a little more alone time." He glanced over at Finn, who was standing up and wiping something off his shirt. "But I understand he's your best friend. I just wish he'd find someone else to hang around sometimes."

Sydney nodded. "I know you do. That's why I'm so happy you're understanding about it."

He pulled her to him once again, and they danced in silence for a few minutes.

"Sydney, you are an amazing person."

Sydney stopped dancing to glance up into his face. Was he kidding?

Seeing the skeptical look in her eyes, he smiled. "I mean it. Look what you've done for Finn. And you really put yourself out there for me, even after the way I treated you in the beginning." He shook his head. "I've never met anyone like you before. You have some magic ability to see into a person and see things they don't even recognize in themselves."

Sydney was shocked. She didn't know what to say. No one had ever thought she was a caring and kind person. Just the opposite, as a matter of fact.

Jeremy frowned. "What's wrong?"

Sydney shook her head. "No one has ever said those things to me before."

"I find that hard to believe."

"No, you didn't know me before I came here. I was not a nice person."

"Okay." Jeremy pulled her back into his arms, and they started dancing again.

"It's true," she said. "I was awful."

Jeremy pulled back, and they kept swaying to the music. He shook his head. "I don't understand how that can be."

Sydney sighed. "I was a lot like you, actually."

"In what way?"

"I was unhappy with my life. My parents were always fighting, and I was mad at them. I took it out on people that had nothing to do with it. I made this one girl's life miserable because it gave me some sort of power. My friends were the same way. They still are. I saw them not too long ago. But I don't want to be that way anymore. I'm so sorry I did it. I wish I could move on from it, but it keeps coming up."

"When?"

Sydney shrugged. "Here and there . . . in conversations with people. I can't seem to shake it."

The music stopped, and Jeremy took her hand. "I have never seen you act that way. I think you've shaken it off and don't even know it."

She shook her head. "But I can never forgive myself for hurting someone."

"Sydney, you have to move on. You're not like that anymore."

She stared down at the floor. "It's still in me, though. I can feel it."

"We all have the capacity to hurt others," replied Jeremy, taking her arm and moving her back to the table. "The trick is not to act on it."

Before she could respond, they reached the table to see Finn arguing with someone.

"What am I supposed to do now?" Finn asked. "I'm soaked! This was a white shirt." He glanced down in horror at the pink stains on the top of his shoes. "And my new shoes . . ."

"I'm so sorry."

Sydney glanced at the young man who was busy trying to mop the table and floor with a few napkins. Jeremy sighed and went to get more, leaving Sydney behind to survey the damage.

"Finn . . . Finn! Stop rubbing your shirt," she said, taking the napkin away. "You have to dab at it, otherwise you'll make it worse."

"Well, what am I supposed to do then?" he asked.

"Go to the bathroom and use cold water to dab at the stains," she advised.

"I don't know . . ."

"Finn, I can't go with you. It's the boys' bathroom," Sydney pointed out. "I'm not going in there."

"I will help you."

Sydney and Finn glanced down to see the boy had moved from the floor to Finn's shoes. He was vigorously wiping the stains and stickiness off. He was so concentrated on his efforts that his hands were stained pink.

Sydney glanced at Finn, who frowned down at the boy. Then he glanced up at Sydney, who was trying to hide her grin at the boy's shoe-cleaning enthusiasm.

"It's not funny," he said sternly, and Sydney nodded, biting her lip to keep from laughing.

Finn looked down at himself and then at the boy on his knees in front of him. He smiled reluctantly.

"I guess it's a little funny. You can get up now," he said to the boy, who stood up and laid the napkins on the table.

"I'm sorry again," the boy mumbled. "I was just going to ask you something, but these are my dad's shoes and I tripped over my feet."

"What were you going to ask?" questioned Sydney as Jeremy returned with more napkins.

The boy looked over at Finn and then glanced at Jeremy. "I was wondering if you wanted to dance," he said, looking at the floor.

When the three of them stared at him silently for too long, the boy stepped back.

"I'm sorry, I shouldn't have asked," he mumbled. "I mean, you probably don't want to anyway . . . ah, I'm going to go now."

"No, wait," said Finn. "Yes."

"Yes?"

Finn shrugged and raised his arms up to look down at himself. "As long as you don't mind my new tie-dyed shirt and shoes."

The boy grinned. "I think you look great. I'm Aiden, by the way."

"I know," said Finn.

Aiden frowned. "Have we met?"

Finn shook his head. "No, but I've seen you around."

Aiden grinned. "It doesn't bother you that I'm—"

"Black?"

"I was going to say 'shorter than you,'" said Aiden.

Finn blushed. "Oh, ah . . . no, that's fine. Sorry about the other . . ."

"Not a problem," said Aiden. "I know I'm Black."

Finn laughed, and Sydney and Jeremy grinned. Jeremy pulled out a chair, and Sydney sat down as Aiden led Finn out onto the dance floor.

Jeremy didn't know what to think. It still made him uncomfortable that Finn was gay, and there he was, dancing with Aiden in front of everyone. He glanced around to see if anyone had noticed, but most people paid no attention. He glanced over at Sydney to see that she was smiling.

"I'm so proud of him for coming out like he did," she said, leaning her arms on the table. "I know how hard it was for him after what his mother put him through." She turned to glance at him. "And you didn't help either."

Jeremy sighed. "I know."

"As far as we all have come in this world," said Sydney, "we have not come far enough."

Jeremy nodded. "I agree. It's too bad, really." He glanced over at her. "You seem to have come a long way."

"In some respects, I have," conceded Sydney. "But I'm still upset about my behavior toward Autumn."

"The girl you gave a hard time to?"

"Yeah. Miikinji', they used to call me."

"What does that mean?"

"Bully."

"Oh." He went silent for a moment, then asked, "Is there some kind of ceremony you can do to make up for things or try to help you forgive yourself for those things? I don't know much about your culture, but they always seem to have rituals for stuff like that."

Sydney glanced over at him and thought about it. "Maybe."

"Well, in the meantime, do you want to dance?"

Sydney nodded, and they went back out on the floor. Several songs later, they returned, laughing and out of breath, to see Finn and Aiden talking at the table.

"Hey, Syd," said Finn. "Aiden here likes old movies."

"Well, good," Sydney replied, sitting down. "Then you can stop dragging me to them. I mean, how many naps do I need?"

"Very funny," grumbled Finn as Aiden laughed.

"Yeah, I'll go with you," Aiden said. "There's a great movie theater called The Parkway. They play older movies, including *Rocky Horror Picture Show*."

"I've heard of that one," said Jeremy. "That's the audience participation one, right?"

"Yeah," replied Finn. "They have a group of people who dress up and put on the show along with the movie. The audience gets to throw stuff at each other."

"Well, something like that, but yeah, it's a great show," Aiden replied, glancing at Finn. "Do you want to go sometime?"

"I don't know," said Finn. "Doesn't that show start at midnight? I don't think my dad will let me stay out that late."

"Well, we can hit another one then," said Aiden. "The others start around seven."

"Are you asking me out?"

"Well, duh."

Finn laughed. "All right. Let's see what's playing, and we'll go from there."

Another ballad came on, and Jeremy asked Sydney to dance. They left Aiden and Finn looking at Aiden's phone and trying to pick out a movie.

Jeremy gathered her in his arms, and she laid her head on his shoulder and sighed. Things were changing really fast with Finn, and she wondered how him dating would affect things.

"You okay?" whispered Jeremy.

"Yes."

"Are you sure?"

"Yes."

He lifted his head and then bent down to kiss her. She wrapped her arms around his neck and held on tight.

Finn took that moment to look up and see their embrace. He watched them for a moment and then looked back at Aiden, who was still trying to get a handle on a good movie for them to go to.

Finn looked around the room, taking in the laughing, flirting, and loud music. It was amazing how complicated life had gotten recently. He remembered a time when he was just a little boy. Life had seemed to be such a simple journey back then. You got up, ate breakfast, and then went out to play. Now it was complicated by friends, family, and dating.

"Finn? Is everything all right?"

Finn turned to see Aiden looking at him, concerned.

Aiden reached out and took his hand. "Is all this going too fast for you? I mean, we went from me ruining your clothes to me asking you out."

"You seem to have everything figured out," said Finn, sighing. "And I don't have a clue what I'm doing."

"Well, right now, we are trying to pick out a movie. But as far as life goes, I go by the 'pick and save' method."

"What's that?"

"You pick your friends well and save your money for a rainy day."

"That seems too simple."

"That's my motto—it doesn't have to be yours. You need to decide for yourself what you want your life to be."

"That's deep."

"That's me," said Aiden with a grin. "The Black Confucius."

Finn laughed.

"So," said Aiden, "let's pick out a movie and solve life's problems on another day, okay?"

"Okay."

Finn gave his hand a squeeze, and Aiden gave him a smile that made him catch his breath. Just then a hard rock song came on the speakers, and Aiden jumped up, tugging Finn out of the chair. Finn laughed as he was pulled onto the dance floor. All serious thought left his head as he struck his disco pose. Aiden laughed, and right there and then, Finn knew it was going to be a good night.

Many Truths

S ydney snuggled into Jeremy's arms in the back seat as his mother drove them home. For once, it was just the two of them. Sydney was a little upset because Finn had disappeared from the dance without saying a word to her.

Jeremy's mother glanced in the rearview mirror but relaxed when she saw they were just talking. She smiled and gave her attention to the road ahead of her.

"Sydney?" asked Jeremy, trying to see her face in the darkened car. "What are your plans after high school?"

Sydney shrugged. "I haven't given it much thought, to be honest. I know Mom wants me to go to college, but I don't like school all that much. I might just get a job."

"I'm going to try to get a football scholarship," said Jeremy.

"Where do you want to play?"

57

"I was thinking of going to school in California."

"California?"

"Yeah."

Sydney pulled away from him and sat up. "So you're not staying either," she muttered.

"What?"

She shook her head. "Why so far away?"

"I have always wanted to go to UCLA."

"Why?"

"It's a good school. My brother went there and—"

"How are we going to see each other?" asked Sydney.

"We have plenty of time to figure all that out," he said with a smile.

Sydney didn't know what to say. She sat back and looked out the window for a moment. "You could stay here," she whispered, but Jeremy heard her.

He shook his head. "No, I want to play professional football."

"They have a team here."

"Not a good one."

Sydney glanced over at him and frowned.

He shrugged. "That's my opinion. And I have always had my heart set on playing at UCLA. My dad went there too, you know." He smiled. "It's kind of a family tradition to go there."

They pulled up to Sydney's house, and she sighed.

"Thanks for the ride," she said to Jeremy's mother, who nodded back at her.

Jeremy got out and rounded the car to help Sydney out. Then he took her hand and led her to her porch door. The light was on, but the shades were closed.

Jeremy glanced back at his mother, who was busy looking at her phone. Then he turned his attention to Sydney. He gathered her in his arms and leaned down to kiss her, aware that her mother could be peeking through the shades or his mother could look up at any second.

After a moment, he pulled away to look into her eyes. She was watching him with an expression he didn't understand.

He frowned. "Is something wrong?" he asked, and she shrugged.

"I didn't know you were going away," she said, looking down at her feet.

"Well, I'm not leaving now, so why worry about it?" he replied, cupping her face with his hand.

She looked up to see him smiling tenderly.

"Inde'," he whispered, and the surprise in her eyes made him laugh. "I looked it up," he said with a grin. "It means—"

"I know what it means," she said softly. "It means 'my heart.'"

He kissed her on the forehead and then squeezed her hand. "Talk to you tomorrow," he said, stepping off the porch.

She watched him leave, not moving from her spot. Even after he and his mother drove away, she stood there on the porch in silence.

After a few minutes, her mother came out. She must have known Sydney was back and been wondering why she hadn't come in yet.

"Sydney?"

Sydney glanced back to see her mother standing in the doorway. She turned away, staring down the street.

Dakotah shut the door and stepped over to her daughter. "Are you all right?" she asked, frowning. "How was the dance?"

For a moment, Sydney didn't speak, and then she turned toward her mother but didn't look at her. "He's leaving," she said quietly.

"Yes, but you'll see him at school."

"I mean he's leaving town."

"Jeremy?"

Sydney nodded.

"When?"

"After high school."

"Where is he going?"

"College." Sydney turned away again. With a sigh, she gathered the small train of the red dress in her hand and sat down on the front porch steps.

"College? Well, that's a few years away. You made it sound like he was leaving right this minute."

Sydney went silent again, and her mother moved closer to her.

"Sydney, what's the matter?"

"He's leaving. And he probably won't be back. He wants to go to UCLA to play football."

"The Bruins," Dakotah said with a smile. "I like that team too."

Sydney didn't answer, and her mother frowned. She moved to the step and sat down next to Sydney.

"What's wrong?"

Sydney sighed and shook her head. "Just another man who's going to leave me."

"What?"

"Dad left. He never came back. I guess he didn't really want me in his life. He's done nothing to change himself so he can see me. I'm nothing to him." She rubbed her eyes tiredly, feeling older than she really was. "They all leave, don't they?"

Dakotah opened her mouth to speak but was cut off by Sydney.

"There are colleges here," Sydney said. "Why can't Jeremy stay here and play? He can still get drafted into the NFL from here. I mean, we have the

Vikings." She shook her head. "He's going to leave
and never come back. I mean, what's the point of
getting involved with him if he's going to leave?"

"What makes you think he won't come back
here? If he cares about you—"

"Dad cared about you once upon a time, and
he still left," Sydney pointed out.

"Not all men leave," said her mother firmly.

"I think so."

"You're young. You haven't had any experience
with men. Jeremy's your first real beau."

"Beau?"

"You know, boyfriend. You can't hold all men
to the same standard as your father. Most men are
better than that. Look at Finn's dad," she pointed
out. "It was Finn's mother who left."

"That is an exception. There are always
exceptions."

"Jeremy could be an exception."

Sydney got up and turned to go into the house.
"Let's face it, Mom. Jeremy's leaving. He's moving
on with his life. He's not going to stay here. He
wants a life someplace else." She opened the door
and then added, "I'm going to break up with him
now. Better to get that heartache over with. Maybe
by the time he leaves, I'll be okay with it."

Her mother stood and touched her arm. "Sydney,
life is not a simple journey. If you care about him,

you have to let him grow. But you can be there right beside him while he does that."

Sydney turned to look at her. "You don't understand, Mom. He didn't ask me to go. He just said he was leaving."

"But maybe he's just trying to figure things out. You should at least talk to him about this a little more."

"Why? So he can break my heart later down the road?"

"That might not happen."

"Things don't work out for us, Mom. The only people we can rely on is each other. Even if he asked me, I wouldn't move halfway across the country and leave you here by yourself." She shook her head. "No, it's better this way. 'Pull the Band-Aid off quick,' you used to tell me. 'The pain will be over with quicker,' you said. With how I treated people in the past and now Jeremy moving away, I am destined to be alone. I will learn to live with that."

Sydney stepped inside, and the screen door clicked shut behind her.

Dakotah stared at the door as several things hit her mind all at once. Number one: Sydney was a teenager and tended to be a little melodramatic. Number two: her father, Roger, had not been a good role model. Number three: she, as Sydney's mother, was not modeling good behavior either. She had not moved on since the divorce. She hadn't dated anyone or even looked in another man's direction. Afraid of being hurt again, she had withdrawn into herself.

With a sigh, Dakotah sat back down on the step and dropped her face in her hands. She had let herself—and worse yet, her daughter—down. She had been taught the Seven Grandfathers' teachings: Love, Respect, Bravery, Truth, Honesty, Humility, and Wisdom . . . none of which she had for herself. There's no way to teach your children things you don't practice yourself.

It was time to go back to her life. She couldn't run away from everything in her past, because some of it was good. She was Anishinaabe, and after everything that had happened, she had forgotten important Ojibwa teachings. She had to get back to the essence of who she was, and so did Sydney.

She got up and headed into the house. She shut the door and went into the kitchen. Picking up her phone, she dialed quickly and held her breath. When someone answered on the other end, she sighed.

"Nokomis, I need you. Can you come?"

Moving On

Monday at school was going along well until Finn threw up in the hall. Sydney had been in class and heard about it from one of Jeremy's friends, who delighted in telling her that "the fag tossed his cookies" in the hall by the gym.

As concerned as she was about him, she stayed away. She was still mad at him for leaving the dance without even telling her. Helping a sick friend was not on her agenda, and Jeremy had practice. She had promised to go watch it after school. *It's time we have a talk,* she thought dejectedly.

After school, she discovered Finn had left a note in her locker saying he was sent home. Sydney took a napkin, moved the note to the garbage can, and then shut her locker door. She would call him later.

As she headed out the side door to the field, the sun hit her eyes, and they watered. She pulled out a pair of sunglasses and put them on. Walking toward the field, she could hear the coach yelling and people laughing in the stands. She found a spot away from the stands in the shade and reached up to remove her glasses.

After a moment, it caught her attention that a group of kids in the stands near her were talking about her.

"Did you see how she's dressed today?"

"Yeah, she's wearing a lot of baggy clothes lately. I wonder if she's knocked up?"

"She could be. You know what a hound Jeremy is. She's just one of many."

Sydney sighed and shook her head. They weren't worth confronting, she decided. But her eyes narrowed as she continued to listen.

"You know, Finn and Aiden left out the side door early from the dance."

"Yeah, I saw that. I wonder where they went."

"You *know* where they went."

"Ew, that's gross."

"Doesn't make it less true," said the girl, pulling her hair up into a messy bun. "Come on, let's go. We're late for cheer practice."

Sydney stepped out of the shade and watched the girls walk around the bleachers, heading for the field. Sydney's gaze darted to Jeremy, who waved. He had been watching her.

She gave him a little smile and then went back to her spot on the grass. Plopping down, she sighed.

As irritated as she was about the girls gossiping, she was more upset with Finn.

When she'd tried to talk with Jeremy about it, he had blown it off, grateful to have her to himself for once. But she had been a little worried about Finn and whatever bad choices he might have been making at that moment. After all, he had made it a point to tell her why people leave the dance early.

Since he was sick and had gone straight home, she couldn't even ask him about it, so she pushed her thoughts about it away. She had bigger issues to deal with as she watched football practice.

She was there to break up with Jeremy. She thought about what she was going to say to him. He'd been so happy the last time he was with her, and he had no idea this was coming. But Sydney knew it was for the best. It didn't make sense to her to have a temporary relationship with someone she knew was eventually moving on.

After about an hour, Jeremy jogged up to her. Practice was over, and he was hot and sweaty.

He plopped down next to her and took the water bottle she offered him. When she nodded, he opened the bottle and downed the whole thing.

"Thanks," he said, taking off his shirt and using it to wipe his face.

Sydney looked away, and he frowned. He set the shirt next to the empty water bottle on the grass and turned to look at her.

"What's up?" he asked.

She took a deep breath and bit her lip. "I . . . I can't see you anymore," she said quickly. "I think we should break up."

Jeremy froze and then frowned. "Why?" he asked.

Sydney shrugged, still not looking at him.

"I think I deserve an answer, Sydney. You just can't dump me without an explanation."

He brought his hand to her cheek. She tried to pull away, but he took her face in both hands and gently made her face him.

"What's wrong?" he asked softly, and tears filled her eyes.

She shook her head sadly. "You're leaving."

He frowned, not understanding for a moment. When she lowered her gaze, he dropped his hands slowly.

"Where am I going?" He shrugged. "I'm not going anywhere."

"You're going to leave the state for college," she said, wiping a tear from her eye. "I don't want to be in a temporary relationship. I think it's best if we don't see each other anymore. It will give us a chance to move on and avoid some heartbreak."

"So, you don't think this is heartbreaking now?"

"Jeremy, you're leaving . . ."

"But not for a few years." He sighed. "A lot can happen in that time."

"What do you mean? You've always wanted to play pro football."

"Yes, but will it happen?" He leaned back on his arms. "Am I good enough? Will I even be able to keep up my college grades so I can play? I mean, you won't be there to help me."

Sydney laughed. "They don't care about your grades, Jeremy. If you're good, you're heading for the pros. They know that."

Jeremy considered that for a moment. "So, I would be going to college for the sole reason of furthering my football career?" He sat up. "I guess I hadn't thought about it that way."

Sydney sighed and then turned to face him. She crossed her legs and sat in what her friends used to call "Indian style." "Look, you are really good. College scouts will be coming to your games at some point. You're going to have your pick of where you want to go." She frowned and looked away. "I don't even know if I want to go to college. I have no idea where I want my life to go yet."

"It's early, Sydney," he replied. "You have plenty of time to figure it out."

"What if I don't?"

"There's no rush."

"Look," she said. "You have your whole life out in front of you. Playing for the pros, endorsements, and lots of money are in your future." She shrugged. "I don't have anything. My mom can't afford for me to go to college. My grades aren't that good, so I won't get any scholarships." She sighed. "I don't really have a future."

"You have a future," he said. "You just don't know what it is yet. There's no rush to have everything set. We're young. We have plenty of time."

"I guess we look at things differently," she said, "because we come from two different places."

"That's what I love about us."

When she snickered and shook her head, he sighed.

"I'm being honest here, Syd. I've never met anyone like you before. If you say you're going to do something, you do it. If you care about someone, you'll go to the ends of the earth for them, like you did for Finn." He smiled. "And how I ended up with you has always amazed me. I mean, I punched you in the face, remember? Not exactly a high point for my social life. What I want to know is, why on earth are you with me? I'm impatient, sometimes unkind, and not that bright. I'm just a sweaty football player who might have some chance at the pros. If not, I may have to become a plumber."

Sydney laughed. "A plumber?"

"Yeah, my dad's a plumber. I may have to fall into that trade at some point." He shrugged. "You're not getting a bargain with me. I will probably let you down a hundred times, and I'm going to be too pigheaded to listen most of the time. But don't give up on me, Sydney. Don't break up with me because you think I'm heading someplace without you." He caught her eyes and smiled. "I don't want to go any place without you. I was never going to leave you behind and go off to college. You can move with me. We can figure this out together. We'll make it work because it has to."

"Why does it have to?"

"Because I don't want to be without you. I'll do whatever it takes to make it happen." He grinned. "You're not breaking up with me, Sydney."

"I'm not?" she asked, crossing her arms.

"Nope. I'm not letting you. For one thing, your reasons are not valid, since I'm not going anywhere without you. I'm sticking to you like stink to a skunk."

Sydney laughed and dropped her arms.

He reached out and took her hand. "We're in this together," he said. "So stop worrying."

She sighed and pulled her hand out of his. She was quiet for a moment and then shook her head. "All men leave. You'll find something or someone better, and you'll go too."

She stood up and brushed off her pants. He stood too.

"You can't lump us all into one group," he said. "We don't all leave. Didn't anything I just said mean anything at all?"

"I know you mean all of this now, but it will change down the road." She shrugged and turned to go. "I want good things for you, Jeremy. Go out there and have a good life without anything to tie you down. I want that for you."

"Sydney . . ."

She shook her head. "Goodbye, Jeremy."

She started to leave, and he took a step toward her. She saw that and put up a hand, and he stopped. She left him standing there as she walked away.

Alone and Lonely

Both Jeremy and Finn were gone from school the next day. Apparently, Jeremy had caught whatever Finn had. Sydney wondered if she would be next.

As she silently moved from one class to another, she could hear people talking behind her back. Word had gotten out about her choice of clothing in the past several weeks, and the word "pregnancy" had been thrown around quite a bit.

To combat that rumor, Sydney had dressed carefully that morning, choosing to wear a ruffled short-sleeved red crop top that showed off her bare midriff, and a pair of black biker shorts that were just long enough for school policy. Her hair was finally long enough for a braid, and she had secured it with a dark brown leather lace. Her black moccasins completed the ensemble. She did not look pregnant.

Things sure had changed. In the past, Sydney would have confronted those people passing the rumors around, but now she walked silently through the halls, ignoring them. They weren't worth her time and energy, she reasoned, quietly noting how big of a change that was for her.

She didn't completely appreciate this new Sydney. She seemed weak and sad, a far cry from the in-your-face persona she used to carry around. But the more she thought about it, the more she understood how stupid that had been. She wouldn't have given Finn the time of day before, and he'd turned out to be the best friend she ever had.

After school, she stopped at her locker to grab her other books and shove them in her book bag. She hoisted the bag onto her shoulders and shut the locker firmly.

"Hi."

Sydney turned around to see Aiden standing there. He was wearing a pair of jeans and a black T-shirt with an alligator logo on it.

"Hello," she answered with a sigh, glancing down the hall.

"You don't look pregnant to me," he said, looking her up and down, and she frowned.

"I'm not."

"I don't know you that well," he said, "but I think that rumor stems from Jeremy. He's been known to not be short of dates, if you know what I mean."

Surprised, she turned to look at him. "I didn't know that," she replied, adjusting her bag on her shoulder. He reached out to take it from her.

"We're heading in the same direction," he said at her raised eyebrows, and he took her arm as they started for the outside doors. "I wanted to talk to you about Finn."

She stopped. "I'm not discussing Finn's personal life with anyone," she said, but he put up a hand.

"Just hear me out, please."

Reluctantly, she started walking down the hall with him. When they reached the doors, he pushed one open so she could go through.

She could see her mother waiting in a line of cars and turned to glance at him. "Well?"

He took a deep breath. "I've heard the rumors about me and Finn. People know we left the dance early. They think we . . ." He trailed off and sighed, and Sydney frowned.

"Where did you go?" she asked. "He didn't even let me know he didn't need a ride home."

"We were together."

Sydney's eyes narrowed. "You hardly know each other."

"No, no . . . it wasn't like that."

"So . . ."

"We had danced a couple of songs and were hot and sweaty. We stepped outside, and three guys started harassing us."

"I didn't know that!" Sydney slowly took the bag from Aiden's shoulder. "Why didn't anyone tell me?"

"A couple of kids saw what was happening and called for Mr. Leehan. By the time he got there, the guys had pushed us up against the wall and were about to start punching. Mr. Leehan stopped them, but the police were called, and we all had to go downtown."

"Why didn't Finn tell me?"

"I don't know. Maybe he didn't have time. He got sick right after, you know." He sighed. "I wondered if he got sick from what happened or if he just had a stomach bug." He shuffled his feet. "He probably never wants to see me again."

Dakotah honked, and Sydney waved away her mother's impatience.

"Look, first of all, this wasn't your fault," she said. "If Finn likes you, it doesn't matter what happened." She smiled. "He won't let that stop him, believe me. He's been waiting for someone like you for a long time."

"You mean someone gay?"

"No, I mean someone who likes him for who he is."

"Oh, I see."

"Look, I have to go," said Sydney. "But I'm going to talk with Finn about all this." She stepped off the steps and turned to look at him. "Look, you guys have to figure all this out on your own. It's not my place to be in the middle of all that."

"Thanks, Sydney," replied Aiden. "If you get a hold of him, tell him I said hello, and I hope he feels better soon."

"I will."

Sydney was starting to walk toward her mother's car when Amelia and her friends sidled up to her.

"Aren't you just the little gay magnet," said Amelia, and her friends giggled.

"I'm glad to see you, Amelia," replied Sydney and gave Amelia's friends a look that made them step back. "I have something to say to you."

"Really." Amelia crossed her arms.

Sydney could see her mother get out of the car and walk around it to stare at them. She also saw Mr. Leehan glance over at them from the sidewalk.

Sydney hoisted her book bag up a little higher on her shoulder and gave Amelia a smile that didn't reach her eyes. "You need to leave Finn and me alone, Amelia," she warned.

"I don't feel like it."

"I was hoping you'd say that." Sydney took a step toward her. "I know you like to think you're better than everyone else, but you are just a low-rent."

Amelia laughed. "What's that? Some Native slang?"

Sydney shook her head. "No, it's someone who has no manners and no class."

"Excuse me?" replied Amelia indignantly. "I—"

Sydney took another step toward Amelia, who stepped back and closed her mouth. They were standing toe-to-toe now.

"People like you have no regard for other people," continued Sydney. "You have no right to talk to Finn, Aiden, or myself. We are head and shoulders above you in every way. You don't deserve our attention. You know, we will grow up and move on from people like you. Unfortunately, you will stay the same hateful person you are now until you decide different."

Sydney turned to go. "I am tired of being harassed by you. If I find out you have caused any more trouble for anyone I care about, you will discover what handling things the Native way means. No one deserves to be treated the way we have been treated by you and your friends. You are no better than the rest of us."

She left Amelia yelling things after her as she got in the car. Mr. Leehan was heading in Amelia's direction as they pulled away. Sydney's mother smiled all the way home.

As soon as Sydney got to her room, she called Finn. The phone rang three times, and then his father answered. When he found out who it was, he put Finn on the phone.

"Hello?" Finn's voice was raspy and told Sydney everything she needed to know. He was truly sick, and it was not just the fight at the dance that had kept him home from school.

"Hi."

"Sydney? Where have you been?" asked Finn tiredly. "I have been trying to call for ages."

Sydney removed the phone from her ear and looked down at it. She had three missed calls from him, but the phone never rang.

"I must have turned off the ringer somehow," she said. "I'm sorry."

"I haven't talked to you since the dance," said Finn, coughing a little. He sighed. "I feel like crap."

"It sounds like it," replied Sydney. "So, how did your night go with Aiden?"

"You mean the dance? It was good," he replied. "He's probably heard by now I threw up in the hall. The school idiots probably couldn't wait to pass that around." Finn coughed harder, and it took him a moment to catch his breath. "He probably doesn't want to see me anymore because of that," he added, wheezing a little.

"Geez, Finn . . . are you going to make it?" asked Sydney, concerned. "Have you been to the doctor?"

"Yeah. He said I had a bug. Should be gone in a few days."

"Jeremy is sick too."

"Oh no. I hope you don't get it."

Sydney nodded. "Me too."

"So, what's going on? I haven't heard from you since the dance."

"I broke up with Jeremy."

"What!" Finn started coughing again, and Sydney could hear his dad in the background telling him to hang up and go lie down.

"I can let you go," she started, but he cut in.

"No, no. Not until you tell me what happened. Did he try something with you at the dance? I knew I should have stayed with you. He has a reputation of—"

"I know, I heard, and no, he didn't try anything."

"Well, something must have happened for you to dump him."

Sydney cringed at Finn's choice of words. "I didn't dump him," she said. "I told him I didn't want to see him anymore."

"Why?"

"Because he's leaving."

"He's leaving?" asked Finn. "Where's he going?"

"To college."

"Now? Man, he's smarter than I thought."

"No, Finn, he's going off to UCLA after high school. He's leaving town."

Finn started to laugh but had to stop because it made him cough again. He took a deep breath and then spoke. "You broke up with him because he might be leaving for college? Where is the wisdom in that?" he asked. "That's crazy, even for you, Syd."

"No, it's not," she insisted. "He's just playing around with me until he leaves. And he's not coming back. He'll get scouted, go to college, and eventually play pro football." She sighed. "No, he's gone."

"Has he given you any indication that he's playing around?"

"What do you mean?"

"I mean, is he seeing anyone else on the side?"

"What? No."

"Has he cheated on you?"

"No."

"Has he treated you disrespectfully?"

"No."

"Did you know he played football when you met him?"

"Yes."

"Did you know he was good enough to be scouted in high school?"

"Well, yes."

"Did you know he wanted to play pro football?"

"Yes."

"Then you knew all this and still went out with him?"

Sydney paused for a moment. "Yes," she admitted.

"Then who's playing who here?"

"What?"

"It seems like you led Jeremy on, letting him think there was some kind of future with you, and all the while you were going to dump him."

"I didn't dump him!" said Sydney loudly. "I let him go."

"Don't you want him anymore?"

"No! I mean, yes. Of course I do. I just don't want to stand in his way."

"Did he say you were?"

"No, of course not. He's too nice."

"So, he dated you to be nice?"

"No. You're twisting my words around, Finn."

"Someone has to," he pointed out. "You're bat crazy if you think he's just playing around here, Syd. The man has real feelings for you."

When Sydney didn't respond, he sighed. "I didn't want to admit that maybe he was a good guy after everything he's done to me and how he's treated me in the past. But I see the way he looks at you when you don't notice. I see the smile he gives you when he spots you across the cafeteria. The man is not playing around. You probably broke his heart when you dumped him."

"I doubt that," replied Sydney quietly. His words were starting to sink in, and she was beginning to wonder if she had made a terrible mistake.

No one spoke for a moment, and then Finn cleared his throat.

"Sydney?"

"Men leave," she said softly. "They don't stay. They have no regard for anyone they leave in their wake either. They just move into your life like gitchi-noodin and then blow out again."

"Gitchi . . . what?"

Sydney sighed. "Like . . . windy, stormy. Men blow in like the wind and then blow right back out again."

"That's what you think of me?" asked Finn softly. "After everything we've been through?"

"No! I was talking about Jeremy."

"I'm a man too, Sydney, just like Jeremy. You can't think we're alike. Jeremy and I couldn't be more different from each other."

"Jeremy can do better than me. He'll find someone else. He'll move on."

"Like your dad did? That's what this is all about, isn't it? You're afraid to trust anyone because he left you."

"He didn't want me, Finn. I have come to terms with that."

"Jeremy is not your father, and neither am I," stated Finn. "We're not going anywhere."

"I know you're not, but Jeremy . . . I just don't believe he'll stay."

"Sydney, you have to have some trust," replied Finn quietly. "If you don't, you will ultimately end up alone for the rest of your life."

Sydney went silent. His words shocked her, and she stopped herself from lashing out at him, trying to hurt him, trying to regain some solid ground in her thinking. In reality, he might be right, and she didn't want to even consider that, because then she would have to let down her guard and be vulnerable.

Finn coughed a little and then sighed. "Just think about what I said, Syd. I love you. You're my best friend. I have always told you the truth. I'm telling you the truth now. Don't throw away everything good you have in your life because some donkey's behind didn't know what he had in his daughter."

When she still didn't speak, he sighed again.

"I have to go now," he said, clearing his throat. "I feel like a truck ran me over. I probably won't be in school tomorrow either. But think about what I said, and we'll talk later. And turn your ringer on this time."

"Okay. Talk to you later."

Finn hung up, and she ended the call on her end and set the phone down. So many emotions were running through her heart, like a swirling, quiet storm. She felt confused and sad. Was Finn right?

Sydney dropped her face in her hands and rocked back and forth. She didn't know what to do anymore.

An hour later, her mother found her on her bed crying. She sat down and pulled Sydney into her arms to comfort her, and neither spoke for several minutes. Finally, Dakotah pulled away to look at her daughter.

"It's time," she said as she caught Sydney's gaze.

"For what?"

Dakotah smiled. "For healing," she said.

"How?"

"It's time for zaangwewe-magooday dance."

Beginning to Heal

S ydney caught her breath and glanced at her closet, which was partly open. She could see layers of copper jingles, each lovingly sewn by Nokomis onto a blue dress. She looked at her mother.

"I called Nokomis," Dakotah said. "I asked her to come. She said no."

"No?"

"She said it is time we heal together. She told me about a powwow in Wisconsin. We will travel there together and dance for healing. Nokomis says it will heal others and ourselves."

Sydney thought about that for a minute. She hadn't danced in quite a while. Not since they left the reservation. "When is the powwow?" she asked.

"This weekend."

"And you will dance too?"

Dakotah nodded. "Yes, I think it is time for both of us to get some healing."

Sydney went quiet again. She thought about her Native traditions and how far they had fallen away from them. They hardly ever spoke Ojibwa anymore and rarely spoke of the reservation.

"I thought the dance was for others to heal," said Sydney. "It seems selfish to dance for oneself."

Sydney nodded. "That was my thought as well. But Nokomis said that in healing others, we heal ourselves as well."

"I don't know if I am in the right place to heal others," replied Sydney softly. "I am broken."

Dakotah's eyes teared up at her daughter's admission. "Me too," she whispered. "We both need healing."

"I thought things were going better for you now that Dad is gone."

Dakotah shook her head. "I am lonely now. I am overwhelmed by responsibility. I went from my father's house to my husband's. I don't know how to take care of myself. And I have you relying on me."

"I'm sorry, Mom, if I am a burden . . ."

"No!" Dakotah pulled her close. "You are the one thing in my life I wouldn't trade away for anything. You are my reason for getting up in the morning."

Sydney thought about that for a moment. What was *her* reason for getting up in the morning? Finn? Jeremy? Her mother?

She shook her head as her mother pulled back. No, she got up because she had to. Not for anyone else, not even for herself.

"I'm not ready to dance for others," she said.

"But the dance will—"

"No, I am not feeling like that will help me. I will be a hypocrite if I try to heal others while I am not well myself. I have to be in the right place in my mind to help others."

"Well, then I have one more suggestion," said Dakotah.

"Okay."

"Let's make a trip over to the American Indian Center in Minneapolis."

"Why?"

"I think we could get some help there. They are one of the oldest Native Indian centers in the US."

"I still don't understand how they are going to help us."

"I'm wondering if they have the Ojibwa Healing Drum Circle."

Sydney knew what that was. But that was for others who had been raped by someone or beaten by their husbands. She didn't understand what that had to do with her.

"Mom, our problems aren't that big," she said. "The circle is for really big problems."

"What you think of as little problems can turn into really big problems," Dakotah pointed out. "And the circle is for anyone who needs healing."

"But we don't know anyone there."

"I think it's about time we connected with people at the center, don't you? There are many Native people living off the reservation." Dakotah got up and walked to the door. "I'm going to give the center a call now."

Sydney watched her mother leave and shook her head doubtfully. There was no way these people were going to be able to help her.

Twenty minutes later, her mother appeared in her doorway.

"They have a drum circle on Saturday," she said. "I told them we would be there."

"Did you tell them why we were coming?"

"No."

"Mother, I still don't think—"

Dakotah put her hand up. "It's for everyone, Sydney. We are going."

"But—"

"Your drum is in my closet in its case. Go get it and make sure the tom-tom is with it."

Sydney left the room and headed down the hall. She went into her mother's room and opened the closet door. Surveying everything in there, she spied her drum bag on the shelf to the left. She carefully pulled it down and sat on her mother's bed to open it up.

It was made of deer hide and was stretched on a wooden frame. Sinew was used to tie everything together, and Nokomis had hand-painted the Four Directions on the drum.

The tom-tom was made from a tree that used to grow in their yard. When its spirit left, it was cut down, and the wood was used for many things. The padded top was made of hide, which was stuffed and then secured with sinew.

This drum was the most precious thing Sydney owned. She slid her hand into the handle in the back and picked up her tom-tom to beat the drum softly as she hummed a tune her mother taught her. Her mother had heard a group called Miiskwaasining Nagamojig, or the Swamp Singers. They sang this song, and she had fallen in love with it.

Sydney started singing it softly.

"Maamawi . . . mashkogaabawiyang
Maamawi . . . mashkogaabawiyang
Anishinaabe ikwewag
Daanisag, anongonsag, noodinag, zaagiwangidwaa
Nibwaachiweyang epiichi nagamoyang
Daanisag, anongonsag, noodinag, zaagiwangidwaa."

Sydney's mother entered the room when she heard the drum. When Sydney finished the song,

Dakotah opened her mouth and started singing, this time in English. Sydney joined in with her drum and voice, and it became a round.

> *"Together we stand strong*
> *Anishinaabe women*
> *Daughters, stars, winds, we love them*
> *We are visiting/conversing/sharing stories*
> *while we are singing*
> *Daughters, stars, winds, we love them."*

As the drumming ended, Sydney and her mother went silent. Then Dakotah gave Sydney a kiss on her forehead as Sydney put the drum back in the bag. Dakotah gave her a nod, and Sydney left for her room, where she set her drum on her dresser.

Pain Is Universal

Saturday came, and Sydney got up and dressed in a blue V-neck shirt and a pair of jeans. Around her neck was an arrowhead necklace her father had given her when she was a child.

After slipping on her black moccasins, she padded down the hall to see her mother shutting the kitchen cupboard door and shutting off the light. She turned to look at Sydney and nodded.

"Let's go," Dakotah said, smoothing down her striped green blouse. She had on a pair of lime-green pants and her brown moccasins. Her hair was pulled back into one thick braid.

They grabbed their drums, and then they left the house, driving west to Franklin Avenue. They arrived fifteen minutes later, and they got out of the car and headed in.

After talking to the lady at the desk, they headed down the hall, drums in hand.

They entered a small room that was warmly lit and smelled of sweetgrass and sage. Dakotah smiled at the woman who greeted them, while Sydney remained silent by her side.

Soon several women arrived with their drums, and Sydney became even more nervous.

"Mom, I think we should go," she whispered.

Dakotah shook her head. Sydney opened her mouth to speak, but just then she spotted a young woman she thought she recognized from school. The young lady walked over to her and smiled.

"Sydney, right? I think we're in math together," she said.

"Ah, yeah, we are."

"First time here?"

"Yeah."

"I know it looks a little intimidating, but no one here bites," she said. "I'm Kendall, by the way," she added, addressing Dakotah now. She reached out for Dakotah's hand and shook it firmly. "I'm Dakota Sioux. My family is from southern Minnesota."

"Nice to meet you," replied Dakotah with a smile. "So the drum circle is for every tribe?"

"Yes," replied Kendall. "Pain is universal. We all need to heal from it."

The group facilitator started gathering everyone together, and they all sat on the floor in a circle with their drums. Sydney sat between Kendall and

Dakotah, acutely aware of the fact that everyone seemed to know everyone else and they were the new people.

"Everything will be fine," said Kendall, leaning over to whisper in her ear. "Don't be nervous. We don't bite the head off of chickens or anything weird like that."

Sydney giggled in spite of herself. "I know that," she said. "I grew up on the White Earth Reservation."

"Oh, okay."

The group leader looked around at each of them as she talked about what the group was about and what they were all there for. No one had to speak if they didn't want to. Everyone would be following her lead throughout the ceremony. Questions were to be saved for after.

She started a slow drumbeat, and everyone picked it up. She started to sing a song that neither Dakotah nor Sydney knew, but it was in Ojibwa.

After the singing and a prayer, bowls of water were passed around. Kendall had one; Sydney did not.

Kendall picked up the cloth that had been laid on the dish and wrung it out. Then she smiled at Sydney and asked her to close her eyes and pray to the Great Spirit for healing. As Sydney did this, Kendall began to wash Sydney's face gently.

At first, Sydney jerked back, but Kendall stopped and quieted her down, and this time Sydney stared into Kendall's eyes as she was being cleansed.

Kendall started to softly sing nanaandawi'iwe-nagamon, and soon Sydney closed her eyes as tears ran down her face. It was a healing song, and Sydney knew Gitchie Manitou could see her pain. For the first time in a long time, she felt as if she wasn't alone, as if she hadn't been abandoned. The water was washing away her tears and her pain over what she had done to others and over her father leaving her. The water was renewing.

After a moment, she opened her eyes to see Kendall holding the bowl of water out to her. She took it, frowning, not sure what to do, but Kendall smiled and closed her eyes to wait.

As she hesitated, she looked down and saw burn marks on Kendall's arms. Some were red and angry, while others were scars that had been there a long time. Her breath caught in her throat as she wrung out the cloth and started washing Kendall's cheeks. She just couldn't imagine the pain this girl had gone through.

Kendall was very still as Sydney washed her face. She was totally relaxed and in the moment, and Sydney was focused on cleansing her pain away.

Sydney started to sing the song she had sung with her mother earlier in the week. A small smile played around Kendall's lips as she listened. After a few moments, Sydney dropped her cloth in the bowl and glanced at her mother.

Dakotah was sitting quietly with her hands in her lap. Her face had been washed, and Sydney could tell she was praying. Sydney glanced back at Kendall, whose lips were also moving in prayer.

Sydney closed her eyes and thought about her father, her mother, Finn, and Jeremy. She thought about her life up to this point and how she had treated everyone in the past. For some reason, she seemed detached from that, as if it was someone else who'd done all that. With a start, she realized that it was someone else.

That wasn't her anymore. She had moved on, grown up, gotten smarter. Her father had left and taken his pain with him. It was not up to her to carry his pain or to let it linger with her.

She also realized she couldn't blame all her insecurities on him. She had allowed things to happen to her. It was only when she stood up to him that he stopped his abuse. She had taken back that power she had so freely given him long ago.

She opened her eyes and glanced at her mother. Her mother had done the same thing. Sydney wondered if her mom was going to be able to move away from the power her ex-husband had to hurt her, and move on with her life. Not all men were like that. Finn said so.

Finn. Her beautiful, wonderful, quirky friend Finn. How lucky she was to have him. She would be forever grateful for what he had brought to her life.

And Jeremy . . . he had done nothing but care about her, and she had walked away. Ashamed now, she dropped her head.

Kendall opened her eyes and looked over at Sydney. She saw the sadness in her eyes and shook her head. "Everything takes time," she whispered. "You have to trust yourself."

Sydney nodded, wiping a tear away.

Sydney sat in silent prayer to the Creator until the group dispersed twenty minutes later. She and her mother headed for their car. Sydney waved at Kendall as she got into her vehicle and shut the door. Kendall waved back.

Sydney and her mother drove in silence, neither wanting to speak. When they pulled into the driveway, both Finn and Jeremy were sitting on the front steps. Dakotah let her out and then parked the car around back.

One Day at a Time

Sydney stood there for a moment, aware the guys were watching her. Then she slowly made her way to the front doorstep.

"Why are you here?" she asked them, and Finn nodded over at Jeremy.

"To protect Jeremy in case you drop-kick him for coming to see you," he said with a grin, and Jeremy shoved him playfully.

Sydney shook her head and waited silently.

Jeremy stood, and Finn got up and started moving toward the backyard.

"I'm going to see if your mom has some bannock," he said. "That stuff is awesome."

Sydney and Jeremy watched him go, and then Jeremy started to speak.

"Syd, I know you don't want to see me anymore, but—"

"Wait." Sydney put two fingers against his lips. She shook her hand and gestured to the stairs.

They both sat down.

"I'm sorry," she said, staring at the ground. "For everything. I never meant to hurt you."

She looked over to see him staring at her, pain clearly in his eyes. But he didn't say anything, waiting for her to go on.

She pushed her hair off her face and sighed. "It's hard to explain, but—"

"Finn gave me the lowdown," Jeremy said. "What I want to know is why you didn't ever tell me how you were feeling or give me the chance to explain." He sighed. "You stood there like you had everything figured out and then dropped me like a hot potato and left."

He shook his head as he went on. "I am so mad at you, Syd. How could you think I was just here for a good time?" He stood up and shoved his hands in his pockets. "I know I was a player before, like, before I met you. But you changed all that for me. I thought you knew that." He turned to catch her gaze. "No, it's not fair what you did to me. I basically told you how I felt about you, and you threw it right back at me and walked away."

Sydney stood and reluctantly faced Jeremy. "You're right. I was wrong. I was wrong about everything, all of it. I blamed everything on my father when it was really me messing things up."

When Jeremy didn't respond, she rushed on. "I'm so sorry," she whispered. "I care about you so much, and I thought there's no way you could ever feel that way about me really, when I don't have anything to offer you in return, and I—"

"Sydney, how can I ever get through to you how much I care about you?" asked Jeremy, frustrated now. "Apparently words aren't going to work here."

The front door opened, and Dakotah and Finn came out to stand beside her. Her mother kissed her on the top of her head, and Finn took her hand in his. Jeremy sighed and looked away.

"I've made such a mess of my life," whispered Sydney.

"True," replied Finn, grinning.

Sydney rolled her eyes.

"But everything can be fixed," he added.

Dakotah turned to look at Jeremy. "If you care about her, give her some time, Jeremy. She's just starting to figure all this out." She smiled at him. "She's worth the wait."

"I am?" asked Sydney.

"Yes, you are," replied Finn.

Jeremy nodded. "She is," he said. "Anyway, I'm not letting you get rid of me, Sydney. But I wish you'd hurry up and figure all this out."

"How is that being patient?" asked Sydney, frowning.

"I never said I was patient," he pointed out. "But I forgive your foolishness."

"My foolishness? I don't think—"

"That's true. You don't."

"Jeremy, that's not very nice to say," said Sydney. "Furthermore, I—"

Jeremy put a stop to any more words by reaching out to kiss her solidly.

Finn rolled his eyes and looked away, and Dakotah's eyes widened. She was not ready to see this.

"Finn, let's go get some lemonade," she said.

"Sounds good to me," said Finn.

Jeremy pulled back and watched them leave. Then he looked back at Sydney, who was frowning.

"Why did you kiss me in front of my mother?" she said. "That was embarrassing, and—"

"No."

"Finn didn't look too thrilled either."

"No."

"And I—"

"No!"

Sydney stepped back.

"I am not going to let you go on and on about why I do stuff," he said. "I did it because I wanted to, and that's that."

"But—"

"Are you going to argue with me every time we're together?" he asked, exasperated.

"Probably."

"Good to know."

They stared at each other for a moment, and then the corners of Sydney's mouth went up. A second later, they were laughing. Jeremy pulled her down on the step and took her hand.

"Jeremy, I still don't have everything worked out."

"I know," he said quietly. "But I can wait. Just don't shut me out anymore, okay?"

"Okay."

They sat on the front step, not speaking, as cars went by, kids played in neighboring yards, and someone mowed their lawn across the street.

Sydney entered a quiet place in her mind. She realized that somewhere along the way she had forgiven herself for what she had done to Autumn. Finn had changed her, and she had let him. And she had finally moved on.

She closed her eyes and raised her face to the sun. She felt the warm rays releasing the tightness in her heart and felt the pain of her past ebbing away.

And for the first time in a long time, she knew she was going to be okay.

ABOUT THE AUTHOR

KIM SIGAFUS is an award-winning Ojibwa writer and Illinois Humanities Road Scholar speaker. She has coauthored two 7th Generation books in the Native Trailblazers series of biographies, including *Native Elders: Sharing Their Wisdom* and the award-winning *Native Writers: Voices of Power*. Her fiction work includes the PathFinders novels *Nowhere to Hide*, *Autumn's Dawn*, and *Finding Grace*, which are the first three books in the Autumn Dawn series, and The Mida, an eight-volume series about a mystically powerful time-traveling carnival owned by an Ojibwa woman. Kim's family is from the White Earth Indian Reservation in northern Minnesota. She resides with her husband in Freeport, Illinois. For more information, visit kimberlysigafus.com.